Before the Storm

Bright Mills

Ukiyoto Publishing

All global publishing rights are held by

Ukiyoto Publishing

Published in 2023

Content Copyright © Bright Mills

ISBN 9789360162061

All rights reserved.
No part of this publication may be reproduced, transmitted, or stored in a retrieval system, in any form by any means, electronic, mechanical, photocopying, recording or otherwise, without the prior permission of the publisher.

The moral rights of the author have been asserted.

This is a work of fiction. Names, characters, businesses, places, events, locales, and incidents are either the products of the author's imagination or used in a fictitious manner. Any resemblance to actual persons, living or dead, or actual events is purely coincidental.

This book is sold subject to the condition that it shall not by way of trade or otherwise, be lent, resold, hired out or otherwise circulated, without the publisher's prior consent, in any form of binding or cover other than that in which it is published.

www.ukiyoto.com

Contents

Beast of the Road	1
Chapter 1	2
Chapter 2	9
Chapter 3	14
Marked For Hatred	18
Chapter 1	19
Chapter 2	23
Chapter 3	28
Killer In The Mist	33
Chapter 1	34
Chapter 2	39
Chapter 3	43

Beast Of The Road

Chapter 1

19-year-old Farida Anand, was spending a holiday with her uncle Mutiu, in Panaji, Goa. She was on her way back to Mumbai, to meet her parents. Panaji is the capital of Goa, and the North Goa district. It is situated on the banks of the river "Mandovi". It is connected to the mainland by bridges. The origin of the name Panaji or Panjim has many explanations. Some of them include it being the corrupted version of "Ponjy" said to mean "the land that never floods". The Portuguese called the city "Panjim" and after liberation, it has seen its name changed to "Panaji". It was a small fishing village with lots of coconut trees, creeks and fields. For centuries, it remained so and was a neglected ward of Taleigao village with the only massive structure, the Adil Shah Fort by the Mandovi river. In 1632 the then Viceroy, Count de Linhares, Dom Miguel de Noronha built the 3.2 km causeway linking Panjim with Ribandar village. It exists even today and is known as the "Pointe de Linhares" and at the time it was constructed, was the longest bridge in existence. Around this time, against the backdrop of the decline of Old Goa, the idea of Panjim becoming the Capital of Goa slowly gained momentum.

On December 1, 1759, the then Viceroy, Dom Manuel de Saldanha de Albuquerque, Count of Ega, shifted his residence from Panelim (near Old Goa) to Panjim. He moved to the newly re-modeled Adil Shah Fort, since known as "Idalcao's Palace". The "Father of Panjim" is a title that is said to belong to the Viceroy, Dom Manuel de Castro de Portugal (1826-1835). He began the process of slowly reclaiming land, initiated public projects, drainage systems and was also responsible for many of its government buildings and set the stage for Panjim to evolve into a magnificent city. By a royal decree on March 22, 1843, its status was elevated to a "City", became the capital of Goa, and was called "Nova Goa". The city was electrified in 1931. Over time, it has undergone many changes under different administrations.

There are two old sections of the city existing today, one called "Fontainhas" and the other "Sao Tome". The hillock overlooking the city is called "Altinho". Today, It is not only the state capital, but also an educational, commercial and cultural center of Goa. The Goa Medical College used to be situated here (since moved to Bambolim) and so do the Goa College of Pharmacy, the Goa College of Art, and the Government Polytechnic. The Dhempe College of Arts and Sciences is situated in nearby Miramar. Some of the important parts of the city are discussed separately in the links below. It boasts of a cultural center-The Kala Academy, and a number of theater complexes.

The main transportation hub is across the "Patto Bridge" over the Rua de Ourem creek at the Kadamba Bus Station. From this Bus station buses take off regularly to other Goan cities like Margao, Vasco da Gama, Mapusa , Ponda and other towns in Goa and to neighboring states. The nearest train station is Karmali, near Old Goa. Typical of a Goan town, Panaji is built around a church facing a prominent square. The town has some beautiful Portuguese Baroque style buildings and enchanting old villas. The riverside, speckled with brightly whitewashed houses with wrought iron balconies, offers a fine view. There are some fine government buildings along the riverside boulevard, and the Passport Office is especially noteworthy. In the 16th century, the edifice was the palace of Adil Shah (the Sultan of Bijapur). The Portuguese took over the palace and constructed the Viceregal Lodge in 1615. In 1843, the structure became the Secretariat, and today it is the Passport Office.

Trudge around town in the cobbled alleys to see quaint old taverns and cafés with some atmosphere, and practically no tourists. They are a good place to meet the local people. The Church Square is a fine illustration of the awesome Portuguese Baroque style. The Church of the Immaculate Conception is easily one of the most elegant and picturesque monuments in Goa. Built in 1541 AD, atop a high, symmetrical, crisscrossing stairway, the church is a white edifice topped with a huge bell that stands in between two delicate Baroque style towers. The Braganza Institute, houses the tiled frieze, which depicts the 'mythical' representation of the colonisation of Goa by the Portuguese. Fountainhas is a lovely old residential area amidst shady cobbled streets connecting red-tile-roofed houses with overhanging balconies, much like a country town in Spain or Portugal. West of Fontainhas, the picturesque Portuguese quarter, the commercial centre's grid of long straight streets fans out west from Panjim's principal landmark, Church Square. Further north, the main thoroughfare, Avenida Dom Joao Castro, sweeps past the Head Post Office and Secretariat Building, before bending west along the waterfront.

The precise and literal meaning of 'lifestyle' is to live life with style that makes its own identity and that is truly distinct from others. And of all the people in India Goan people have all the right to take lot of pride for having developed a lifestyle that is unique and one that truly expresses their cultural heritage. A unique culture and lifestyle where everything mingles, where conservative Indian sarees seamlessly treads with western attires of swim suits and miniskirts, where religion of east and west fuses together beautifully and where people simply live their life as it comes. These are few important traits of Goan people's lifestyle, which has been in practice since many centuries.

And nowhere is this typical Goan lifestyle of tremendous diversity more visible than in capital city of Panaji. As this city is by far the best exponent of Goan lifestyle. Here people have surely lapped up modern values, but not at the cost of traditional Goan lifestyle. And this is exactly the reason why local people here don't at all hesitate in wearing modern designer cloths, where also other symbols of modern consumerism like spas, fitness gyms and beauty salons do amazingly roaring business. And all these progressive signs of modernity seamlessly live aside with sheer simplicity that Panaji people still haven't forgotten. The simple cloths like shirts and trousers, the conservative Indian sarees and salwar kameez still troll on the streets of Panaji city.

But, all said and done about Goan people's amazing ability to accept diversity, there is another aspect of Goan people's lifestyle which is equally beautiful. And that is there laid back attitude towards life, to simply live life as it comes. This chilled out attitude towards life is visible and felt throughout Goa, more so in the city of Panaji. Here people do not try to run faster than life, because they love life so much that they live every moment as it comes. Here relishing the Goan music, enjoying delicious Goan cuisine, strolling on a beach, playing beach football, waiting for New Year party with bated breath has always taken precedence over earning fast money. The sheer love for life that Goan people have is such a fresh breadth of air in today's era of globalization where people's maddening love for money has taken precedence over love for life itself.

To sum it up, the life of Goan people is that of pure love for everything beautiful that makes up human life so enjoyable, in other words: to love diversity of life to the fullest. It is indeed this colorful lifestyle of Goan people that today makes it one of the most cosmopolitan and multi cultural places in India. And also, one of the most beloved tourist destinations of this country. Panaji - is a charming blend of modern India and the country's classic roots. It is surrounded by green, terraced hills and overlooks the Mandovi River. With cobblestone streets and colorful villas that date from the Portuguese colonial period, a Latin quarter, and floating casinos on the river, the capital of the state of Goa offers a variety of experiences for a small city of just under 115,000.

The city is home to many examples of graceful architecture, including the ornate Our Lady of Immaculate Conception Church and the bright orange Maruti Temple. A Quiet Culinary Capital: Without a lot of fanfare, Panjim has a centuries-old culinary tradition that results in world-class dining options, including spicy traditional Goan cuisine and Portuguese favorites leftover from colonial days. With the bounty of fertile agricultural lands and the rivers and oceans nearby, the food is fresh and flavorful at popular restaurants like Viva Panjim and Daawat. At the foot of the Altinho Hill, the Latin Quarter or Fontainhas was established by a Portuguese colonialist in the late 18th century. It retains much of its Portuguese character and could be mistaken for a Mediterranean town, with its many red-tiled roofs and narrow streets. Panjim is set in a green, fertile area that can be explored in a variety of ways, including exciting jungle excursions. There are numerous hiking and trekking options, with many local guides and operators available to help.

From golden beaches to cruises and boat tours, the rivers and nearby Arabian Sea are waiting to be discovered. World-class scuba diving and barracuda diving are also available for the more adventurous. Miramar Beach on the Arabian Sea is made up of soft, golden-colored sand dotted with palm trees. It's a popular escape from the city for visitors and locals alike. Dona Paula, another beach, lies just outside the city where the Zuari and Mandovi rivers meet. Many Bollywood films have been shot there. Ashwem Beach is a third, and often less busy, option nearby in North Goa District. India's only legal casino is also a cruise boat on the Mandovi River. Casino Caravela offers a variety of gaming choices, including American Roulette, with sightseeing along the river to take up any down time.

This large center includes many exhibits and interactive installations and is located near the Miramar Beach. There is also a 3D movie theater that screens interesting educational science films. Along with taking walks in the lush surrounding area to enjoy the natural setting, the Salim Ali Bird Sanctuary is located nearby in the village of Chorão. It houses a large collection of exotic and rare birds in a beautiful natural setting. Old Goa is just 6 miles from Panjim. Once the colonial capital of Goa State, is is full of ornate old churches and other historic buildings that have been well maintained. Old Goa is listed as a UNESCO World Heritage site.

On March 15, 1991, Farida Anand hit the ride from a truck driver as a lift. The truck driver Krish Ahuja, was heading towards Kohima. After a few hours on the road, she fell asleep at the back of the truck. The truck driver thinks that is exactly what he was waiting for. He stopped the truck by the roadside, got to the back of the truck and over powered Farida. Before she was fully awake Krish chained her against the wall at the back of truck and raped her. She was chained inside the truck for six days. The ordeal did not end there. Krish took her to his Panaji apartment and allowed her to bathe, then chained her to the bed and raped her several times. She watched helplessly as he approached her with a razor blade and began to slides off her hair. After eight hours of assault he forced her back into the truck. This time, he fails to bind her. When he stopped at the gas station to buy some gas and some beer in the shopping mart at the gas station, he left her alone and walked inside the shopping mart.

Farida knew this might be her only chance to escape. She ran for it, still having the chains on her hands and neck. She ran very far stopping vehicles passing by for help until a vehicle stopped and took her to the police station. Farida told the police that she had been kidnapped, tortured and raped, but she managed to escape. She gave the description of the truck driver and the truck to the Panaji police officers. The police patrol team was searching for the truck and the driver on the high way. The police stopped a truck in that area that fits Farida's description. The police took him to Farida at the station and showed her the truck driver if he was the one that attacked her, but she said no. It was indeed Krish Ahuja, the truck driver that abducted and raped her. But Farida was scared to tell the police the truth. She did not want to press charges but wanted to go home. The background check of the truck yielded no warrant for conviction so the police released the truck and the driver. Farida was too frightened to testify against the attacker, so the police let her go.

On April 10, 1991, after Farida's incident, another young lady was in the high way looking for a ride. Just 13 miles away from Panaji, a 15 year old Sarika Patel, was running away with her new boyfriend, Akash Bhatt. Her parents were divorced, and she usually stay with her father in Panaji. She did visits her mother, Sita Patel for a few days, when she fled with her new boyfriend. The trucker soon stopped for the pretty young lady and her boyfriend. She and her boyfriend entered into the truck. Sarika mother Sita, was a single mum, who worked for long hours as a department store clerk. When she came home from work, she was surprised to find out that her daughter was not at home. She called her name several times to see if she was somewhere in the house but her daughter did not answer. Sita saw no note and no other sign that her daughter has been back to the house.

She checked the answering machine but Sarika has left no messages. Sita called her daughter's friend and Sarika father in Panaji. But neither of them knew her where about. She then reported to the police that her daughter is missing. She spoke with a police officer in the juvenile section, giving her Sarika's description. The 15 year old daughter was about 5 feet tall, weighed 95 pounds, and have long curly dark hair. The detective asked Sita what steps she has taken so far to find her. Sita has posted missing persons flyers, but no one has yet responded. The worried mother had not heard from her daughter since they argued two nights before. At 10:20 that night, Sarika told her mother that she was going to visit a friend. But Sita objected, but Sarika insisted that she will be right back. Against her better judgement, Sita relented. Trusting Sarika will come back home.

Though the young teen has a history of running away. She always returned on her own. Her believe this time is different. Police detective Jaya Reddy, of the juvenile division was assigned the case. She understood Sita's concern. Several days past and Sarika would normally calls the mother when she leaves home. Sita posted more flyers on various stores. She held out hope that her daughter was unhurt. She thought maybe she would simply stay with a friend. Alone with Sarika's photograph and description, Sita offers a reward for information of her daughter's where about.

Chapter 2

Five days after Sarijka's disappearance, Sita receives a phone call. The caller has seen Sarika talking to two young men on the evening she left her mother's house. The person only knew the men were Sajan Babu and Samay Bakshi. But she remembers that Sajan has a girl friend with a peculiar name of Vidica Verma. Sita immediately called the police. The following day a second call gave Sita the address of an apartment where he has seen Sarika two days before. When the police got to the apartment the Land Lord told them that the apartment was rented to a man called Sajan Babu. The next morning detective Jaya Reddy told her colleagues about the case. She mentioned she was looking for Sajan Babu, in connection with Sarika's disappearance. She was also looking for two others. A woman named Vidica Verma and a man named Akash Bhatt. She did not know their last names. To her surprise, the officers did. Sajay has a girlfriend name Vidica Verma, and her friend's name is Akash Bhatt. The three were wanted in connection with an auto theft. Units were dispatched to each department to wait for his return. Police officers patrol the nearby road.

After several hours of surveillance, they picked up 18 year old Sajan Babu and his girl friend Vidica Verma near his apartment. The police handcuffed him and brought him to the station for questioning. The third suspect Akash Bhatt was still at large. The police asked Sajan if he has seen Sarika and Akash Bhatt. Sajan said he has spoken with them four days ago, but have not seen them. He told the police that Akash and Sarika were in love and plan to run away to Nepal where Akash have relatives. The detective suspected that Akash has another reason for leaving town. Sarika was 15 at that time with her boy friend. When they saw the flyers Sita had placed on various places about Sarika disappearance, they both decided to flee to Nepal. The detective leant that Akash is already in a probation for theft.

The police issued a warrant for his arrest. Detective Jaya also fed Sarika's description into the Indian Crime Database nation wide. If Sarika is located anywhere in the country, the Panaji police will be notified. Until then, with no known address of vehicle, it will be difficult to find the girl. 16 miles away, the police interviewed Sai Patel, Sarika's father. He told the police that he received a disturbing call on the evening of May 18. He did not recognized the caller's voice. The caller asked, are you Sarika's father? Sai Patel replied, yes. The caller told himthat he knew where his daughter is. He said that he kept the girl somewhere. Sarika's father asked if she was dead or alive. But the caller hang up the phone. Detective Jaya asked the police to track the call. The phone company said it will take several days. The police simply have to wait. Besides from the phone record, the trail of the missing 15 year old and her boyfriend were stone cold. In May of 1991, detective Jaya continue her search for 15 year old Sarika. The girl has not been seen since early March, when she left her friend's house with her 18 year old boyfriend Akash.

The detective only lead was the anonymous phone call made to Sarika's father on May 18. The call that is yet to be traced. On the saem night when Sarika's father received his call in Panaji, her mother in Panaji also got a call. She recorded the conversation as the police has advised. An unknown man told Sita to meet him at 7:30 next morning at a local convenient store, that he had something to tell her about Sarika, and wanted to say it in person without giving his name of description, he hang up the phone. Sita called detective Jaya and told her that it was risky to meet the man. Sita insisted that the detective will go with her for protection. From a distance police officers kept an eye on Sita as she waited at the local convenient store for the unknown caller. She has no way to identify him. Her only hope is if he will approach her. She studied everyone that came in and out and uses the pay phone. Sita waited over two hours. The caller never came forward.

Two days later, detective Jaya received the phone records for both calls. She learned that the phone call made to Sai Patel was made from a gas station, 200 miles North West where Sarika was last seen. The call to Sita's home was made from a pay phone only a few blocks away. At that particular time, it was obvious that the police was very concern about Sarika's where about. With the phone calls and the information that the police has received, the police was pretty sure that there is going to be a foul play involved. Two weeks later Sita told Jaya that the man who had called her before wanted to set up another meeting at the same convenient store. The police traced the call to a nearby pay phone, but the caller had already fled. On April 25, the police found a small skeleton of a female in a river bank, in Panaji, Goa. They determine the young girl age and weight was close to Sarika.

Detective Jaya brought Sarika's record to the medical examiner. They mase a comparison and found out that the deceased was not Sarika. Months have passed with no news. Sarika's parents feared the worse. On November 15, two boys were playing in a bush path close to the road, they came across a wood pile. They found something they will never forget. It was a human remains. They ran home to tell their parents and called the police. Polices officers arrived at the scene and secured the area. They could not identify the body at that sight. The body was so badly decomposed. All the police could guess was that the victim was a child or a young adult. They hope the autopsy will tell them more. Detective Jaya took Sarika's records to the police laboratory for comparison and investigation, but they did not matched.

The police was very disappointed but relieved that it was not Sarika. Sarika parents are beginning to think that at this point, the police are looking forward to recovering Sarika's dead body and that she is no longer alive, and were ready for some type of closure at this point. As the search continues in Panaji, through the fall in 1991, a farmer prepare to burn down his old barn in the state of Nagaland. He had not been inside in years. The farmer climbed up the stairs inside the barn to make one last check of the place. He looked through the abandoned building, but found items long discarded. Nothing seems special or unusual were out of place. Then something caught his eyes. He looked closer and saw skeleton that seems to be human.

The farmer immediately called the police. In October of 1991, as detective Jaya hunted for 15 year old Sarika, a decayed body was found inside a barn in Nagaland. Detective Ajay Dara of the Nagaland state police responded to the scene. Crime scene technicians conducted a thorough search of the barn. No cloths was found on or near the body. There was no wallet and no other ID. They did found a single white tread close to the bone, that seems new to be in the bones. The police photographed the remains from various angle. They found bailing wire that matched the wire wrapped around the neck of the deceased. Some hair remains on the head. Because the skull was so small, police believe the victim was probably a child. The people living in that community have not seen a murder for ten years. The anonymity of this crime is very disturbing. The police have no way of knowing if the victim is from the area. Forensic pathologist was called to carry out ab examination.

He made several discoveries that helped detective Ajay Dara to start identifying the body. Ajay was able to identify that it was a young female between the ages of 14 to 16 and approximately weighs between 90 to 100 pounds. There was an indication that her hair has been cut. The cause of death was determine to be strangulation. The killer almost severed the victims head. He puts a bailing wire around her neck. It was also noted that the girl was killed almost a year before. The forensic scientist analyzed the white fiber found around the body. They discovered the fiber is made from cotton and did not come from clothing. It is likely it came from a towel. Detective Ajay searching the Indian Crime Database listed the Nagaland that a white female, 14 to 16 years of age, probably killed as early as September 1991. There were about 900 matches with the age group in the category and period, which makes it difficult to begin the identification process. He then sent text messages to all police station about the victim for further identification. Detective Jaya, investigating the disappearance of Sarika Patel, got her own copy of the text message. She believes the body description fits Sarika Patel. She phoned the police at Nagaland. She remembered the mysterious phone called Sarika's father received of which the caller told him that Sarika is in the barn. Therefore, she ask the Nagaland police if the body was found in a barn, and they said yes. She immediately concluded that it could be Sarika Patel's body. Jaya travelled to Nagaland with the records of Sarika for comparison. After thorough comparisons and investigation, it was discovered that the victim's body was Sarika Patel. The question now is where Sarika's boyfriend is. The detectives called on the Indian Special Task Force for help.

The special task force went contacting and interviewing anybody that has anything to do with Sarika or Akash. They went to Akash high school and the police were told that he had not been coming to school for nearly a year. The police collected his house address from the high school. They went to his parents' house where he lives with his parents but met his sister Divya Bhatt. Divya told the police that no one in the family has seen Akash for over a year. They have written him off as a bad kid believing he will end up in prison. The detective asked if they have relative in Nepal. She said yes. They showed Divya Sarika's photo if she has seen her before, but she said no. The special task force believes that Akash did not commit the crime, because he would have done it in a fatal angle. They said the suspect is likely to be an older person, probably a traveler or a truck driver driving across the state. The investigatots was informed about another crime in Panaji. Just 200 miles North of Panaji, partial skeleton remains of a young man was found washed up in a quick bank.

The skeleton has been proliferated on the left side by a firearm. However, there was a little evidence to positively identify the body. The victim age and location led police to conclude that he was probably Akash Bhatt. To the investigators, it looked like the man who killed Sarika and Akash has gotten away with murder. As the hunt for the killer grant to a halt in Panaji. Thousand mile west of Mumbai, a police patrolling came across a truck packed by the roadside on the high way. He climbed the head of the truck to see who was inside and what he saw terrified him. He saw a woman a woman handcuffed and chained to the wall at the back of the truck crying and screaming for help while the truck driver was busy assaulting her. The police immediately ordered the driver to come out of the truck. The driver was telling the police officer that there was no problem, that they were just having fun.

Chapter 3

However, the police did not believe him because he could hear the woman's voice inside the truck screaming for help. He arrested the truck driver, handcuffed him and put him inside his police vehicle. He then went to the truck to check on the woman and found the woman handcuffed and chained to the wall of the truck crying and screaming for help. The police immediately called for backup. The police backup team quickly arrived and free the woman. They took her and the truck driver to the police station for questioning. Inside the truck the police found different types of torturing tools, along with a camera and women's hair. The victim was a 28-year-old Nila Basu. She told the detectives that she has been picked up an hour earlier by the truck driver pretending to be giving her a lift. When she slept off, the trucker handcuffed and chained her to the wall of the truck and started assaulting her. The police photographed all her injuries. The detective asked the trucker Krish Ahuja, for his own side of the story. Krish said that Nila was crazy and that she solicited him and he did not have sex with her. He refused to provide any further details on what happened in the truck.

He talked around the subject but never admitted ao any crime. The police photographed Krish wound that Nila had on him. Nila bit him on the shoulder as he was assaulting her. Krish denied that he sustained the injury while loading his truck, but the detectives did not believe him. The police arrested Krish for sexual assault and unlawful imprisonment on Nila Basu. Nevertheless, the police only witness Nila, suffers from paranoid delusions. To keep Krish behind bars, the police needed an additional witness. Nila claims Krish has been kidnapping and raping women for over 15 years. The detectives wrote Krish Ahuja's name into the Indian Crime Database and place it on other agencies that have reported similar crimes. As the detective pursue the case, they made headlines across the South West of the country. The Panaji police officer was among those who read about it.

The police suspected that the truck driver was the man who held Farida captive for six days raping and torturing her until she finally escaped. They were unable to press charges on Krish because Farida could not identify him. The Panaji police called the Mumbai police and described the case to them. The Mumbai police started suspecting that Krish is a serial rapist and might even be a murderer. The police then contacted the Indian Special Task Force for assistance. The police hope with the special force support they can gather enough evidence for the truck driver sex crimes to build the case. The special force checked the truck driver apartment and were terrified to find different types of torturing devices. They also found handcuffs, lots of women jewelries, bloody white towels, women's clothing and lots of photographs. They then concluded that Krish is a serial rapist.

By December 1991, the best Mumbai police could do was to offer Krish a deal, which is six years including time serve, work release eligibility, if he pleads guilty to the crime against Nila Basu. The reason is that the police still needs additional witness. The case will be he said and she said, and that might left the jury unconvinced. The special task force found Sarika's photo in Krish apartment. They started building a kidnap and murder case against the truck driver Krish Ahuja. They also saw Sarika's cloths and jewelry in Kirish apartment. They also discovered that the cotton fiber found on Sarika's skeleton was from the bloody towel found in Krish's apartment. But the result was so inconclusive because that types of towel was very common. They also discovered that Krish got Sarika's parents phone number from her notebook found in his apartment. Flipping the notebook the special force found something even more disturbing.

A letter written by Krish Ahuja himself stated, "Akash Bhatt is a dead man". So the special force were waiting for a DNA report to confirm that the remains and skeleton of the young man found was Akash Bhatt. But unfortunately they could not get the DNA of the skeleton. The special force then checked the crime database to see more crimes that might have been committed by the truck drive Krish Ahuja. They were surprised to discover 50 similar crimes of kidnappings, torture, rape and murder. They discovered that he has been abusing and killing people in remote locations during his trips with his truck. The special force went again to search Krish truck and found some hair that is believe to come from Sarika Patel. They also found Sarika's finger prints on the wall of the truck where she was handcuffed and raped. That proved that she has been in the truck but cannot prove when or whether she has been there against her will.

By January 1993, almost two years after Sarika has disappeared, investigators determine the evidence was not decisive enough to prove a case of kidnapping. They drop the federal case. But the investigators decided to press charges for capital murder. They knew the evidence was circumstantial if they press charges. The detective fears that if they did not get enough concrete evidence against the truck driver he could be released. On February 8, 1993, the investigators traveled to Mumbai prison to serve the warrant to Krish Ahuja. The plan is to confront photographs of Sarika to Krish, hoping to prompt him to confession. But Krish was unwilling to speak with them and denied any involvement in the death of Sarika and Akash Bhatt. At that point the detectives knew that they have to prove their case. Krish knew that the investigators wanted him to confess because their evidence was weak.

The truck driver was transferred from Mumbai to Panaji to face his trial in the law court. The detective succeeded in prolonging the judgement for six months so that they can gather enough evidence. They contacted again the Indian Special Task Force for help. The task Force visited Krish apartment again this time with a sniffer dog. The dog led them to an astonishing discoveries. They found lots of photographs of people Krish had assaulted and murdered inside a carton hidden inside his roof. These includes 50 victims including Sarika and Akash. They also found the hairs of these 50 victims and a video camera he used in videoing his victims during torture before killing them. This was the straw that breaks the camels back. The gave all these evidence to the investigators who jubilated like having a Christmas party. The investigators were able to made Farida Anand to identify Krish Ahuja as the man that kidnapped, tortured and raped her after showing her all the evidence they have gotten against Krish, making her to understand that if they should let him go free, he is going to commit more crimes. And that she should cooperate with them to take him down.

Farida agreed and did testified against Krish in the law court. Krish was faced with concrete evidence that he could no longer denied. He was found guilty by the law court of kidnapping, torture, rape and murder againg Sarika, Akash and 48 other victims. He was therefore sentenced to life in prison. Krish Ahuja almost got away due to not enough concrete evidence against him at first, but thanks to the brilliant performance of the Indian Special Task Force.

Marked For Hatred

Chapter 1

At the Imphal airport, on Monday, January 28, 1997. An airline took off from Imphal, Manipur, to Mumbai. A 57 year old Arjun Khatri, was on board. Arjun was operating a bus transportation company in Imphal, Manipur. He has made millions and he is on his way to Mumbai to meet a new industry contact. Imphal is the capital of Manipur and a famous tourist destination with historic places and tourist spots. On 18th June 1997, Imphal district was split into Imphal East and Imphal West with different district headquarters. The architectural forts, the historical places and the green valleys and hills surrounding the town present a beautiful and mesmerizing sight for the tourists. Imphal is bordered by the Thoubal district, Senapati district and the Bishnupur district of Manipur. The town of Imphal was originally ruled by Kin Khaba and later by the Pakhangba rulers. It is through this that a powerful Ningthouja dynasty originated and ruled. After the Ningthouja tribe, the British took over and ruled in Manipur. During that period, wars like the Anglo Manipur war took place due to internal differences between the members of the family.The war also took place between the people of Manipur and the British. However, the British won and Manipur came under the British rule until Independence.

The present day Imphal is developing at a fast speed. The government has made all the endeavors to develop the city in terms of economy, culture, education and transportation providing basic amenities to the people. Imphal is gradually becoming one of the most popular tourist destination of northeast India. Click here for more information on history of Imphal. Imphal is located at an altitude of 786 meters above sea levels, in the extreme east of India. Many rivers like the Iril, Khuga, Thoubal orginate from the hills surrounding the valley of Imphal. The climate of Imphal is tropical or humid subtropical in nature. The summers hot and humid and winters are cool and dry.The temperatures range from a minimum of 4° C to a maximum of 25° C.

The average rainfall of Imphal is 1320 mm. Click here for more information on geography of Imphal

Manipur through its rich arts and culture has been identifying itself to the people living in India as well as abroad. The Manipuri people are very much fond of music and dance and it is very difficult to find a Manipuri girl who cannot dance or Sing. Manipur is world famous for its manipuri style of classical dance. Manipuri handloom and handicrafts also depicts the rich culture of the people of Imphal. The important festivals celebrated in Imphal include Ningol Chakouba, Yaoshang, Kang, Heikru Hitongba and many more. Imphal situated at height of 790 m. above the sea level is a beautiful tourist place with tripling rivers, cascading rapids, varieties of flowers, exotic blooms and lakes. The city of Imphal is endowed with many beautiful tourist destination. Thousands of tourists, every year visit the place to enjoy the nature and beauty. The Shaheed Minar is located at Bir Tikendrajit Park in the heart of the city of Imphal. Another very important tourist spot in Manipur is the Kangla. This place is the historical embodiment of Manipur Rulers. Loktak lake, located 48 kms from Imphal is a must visit tourist place in Manipur. This lake is the largest fresh water lake in North East India. Other Important tourist place in Imphal include Shree Shree Govindajee Temple, Manipur State Museum, War Cemetery, Manipur Zoological Garden, Khonghampat Orchidarium, Sadu Chiru Waterfall, Keibul Lamjao National Park and many more.

The tourist must make it a point to stroll along the busy market areas in Imphal and to pick some great souvenirs to take back home. The bazaars in Imphal are mostly occupied by women and this market gives you a glimpse of the Manipuri Culture and tradition. Khwaraimbad Bazaar in Imphal is one of the most famous and largest women's markets in India. From silk saris to hand-woven shawls, footwear to colorful attires, vegetables to spices the markets in Imphal have it all. The popular markets in Imphal are Khwairambad Bazaar, Paona Bazaar, Tera Bazaar, Nagampal Market and GM Hall. Imphal has a well developed transport system. The Imphal International Airport is the major airport and the 2nd international airport in the northeat region after Guwahati. There is no railway station in Imphal but NH-39 links Imphal with railhead at Dimapur in Nagaland and NH 53 links Imphal with railhead at Jiribam. Imphal is also well connected by roads. The Impahl west district is connected with Guwahati through the National Highway 39 to Silchar through the NH53. The National highway 39, 53 and 150 connects Imphal East district to other places of northeast.

Imphal was the seat of the kings of Manipur before the region fell under British rule. In 1944 it was the site of a significant tactical victory for the Anglo-Indian forces over the Japanese on the Burmese front of World War II. The city is a major trade centre noted for its weaving, brass-ware, bronze-ware, and other cottage industries. Imphal College, Imphal Training Centre, Dhana Manjari College, and a technical school are located there. Imphal is connected with the North-Eastern Railway at Dimapur, Assam, and with Myanmar (Burma) by hard-surface roads. It has an airfield with regular service to Kolkata (Calcutta; 400 miles [650 km] west-southwest) and Guwahati in Assam state. About two-thirds of the people are Meitei (Meetei), who occupy the Manipur valley and are largely Hindus. Meitei women conduct most of the trade in the valley and enjoy high social status. Indigenous hill tribes, such as the Nagas in the north and the Kukis in the south, make up the rest of the population. Divided into numerous clans and sections, the people of these tribes speak languages of the Tibeto-Burman family and practice traditional animist religions. Some of the Nagas have been converted to Christianity. More than three-fifths of the people speak Manipuri, which, along with English, is the official language of the state. Manipur's population is largely rural, Imphal being the only city of any size.

Agriculture and forestry are the main sources of income. Rice is the major crop, and the rich soil also supports corn (maize), sugarcane, mustard, tobacco, orchard fruits, and pulses (legumes). Terracing is common in the hills, where the farmers plow the ground with hand hoes. Among some of the hill tribes, domestic animals are kept only for meat and are not milked or used for hauling. Teak and bamboo are major forestry products. The Nagas are known to use intoxicants to catch fish. Manufacturing is limited to several well-established cottage industries. The designed cloth produced on hand looms is in demand throughout India and outside the country. Other industries include sericulture (silk production), soapmaking, carpentry, tanning, and the manufacture of bamboo and sugarcane products. An industrial complex, including an electronics plant, has been established at Imphal.

About three-fifths of the population is literate; the state has a university at Imphal and more than 30 colleges. Major health problems include tuberculosis, leprosy, venereal disease, and filariasis. The state continues to have an inadequate number of health facilities. Polo and field hockey are popular sports. Manipur has given birth to an indigenous form of classical dance known as manipuri. Unlike other Indian dance forms, hand movements are used decoratively rather than as pantomime, bells are not accentuated, and both men and women perform communally. The dance dramas, interpreted by a narrator, are a part of religious life. Themes are generally taken from the life of Krishna, the pastoral god of Hinduism. Long an isolated art form, manipuri was introduced to the rest of India by the poet Rabindranath Tagore in 1917.

Chapter 2

Arjun Khatri told his family and co-workers that he would be home on Monday for another meeting. He also told them that his contact in Mumbai, a woman name Navi Dalal, was to pick him up at the airport. She will take him to meet others in the lucrative business deal. Privately, Khatri hope to retire after closing the deal. When Khatri fails to return on Tuesday, his family contacted the Imphal police. Detective Sergeant Ari Amin was one of the state detective assigned the missing person's case. Arjun is the kind of person that will always phone home; always want to know what is going on with his business. Without Arjun the business did not run. That is why they were concern why they did not hear from him. He suddenly disappeared. Arjun is not that can of person that will just walk away from his business. Imphal investigators interview Arjun's daughter Uma Khatri and his girlfriend and office manager Meera Chadha. Uma said her father missed an important meeting about the sales of his business. He also has not answered calls to his phone. Meera recalls that the woman from Mumbai, Navi, has phone the office many times recently but never left her number. The Mumbai woman claims to represent a company called Kalpen exporting. Navi provides a description of herself so that Arjun could recognized her at the airport.

She said she was 5 feet one and blonde-haired person. The detective visits the travel agency who booked Arjun's flight. The agency confirmed that Arjun purchased a one-way ticket to Mumbai. He did not bother to rent a car since his contact is coming to pick him up. Airline record collaborated that Arjun has bought the flight. But he has not registered at any hotel upon his arrival in Mumbai. An examination of Arjun record reveals that his credit card has been used after his arrival in Mumbai. To follopw the credit trail, Imphal detectives contacted the law enforcement. Rishi Bakshi was assigned the case. They discovered that Arjun credit card was used at the Hilton International Hotel, Mumbai, between approximately 1:00am – 2:00

am. From January 28 to January 29. And then at 4 O'clock in the morning, another of his credit card was used to purchased gas, at the gasoline station in North Mumbai. To the investigators, this seems odd, since he had not rented a car.

The detectives interviewed the employees at the gas station who have worked on January 30. They showed the fuel attendants the photograph of Arjun but they could not recognized him. The gas station punched all credit card slots. The employees could not recall any one fitting Navi Dalal's description. The detectives contacted the law enforcement for the address of Kalpen exporting. They found no such company registered in the state. They also intended to locate Navi Dalal herself. On February 1, the detectives in Imphal state police, travelled to Mumbai. Nobody have heard from Arjun in five days. Detectives now believe the millionaire have met with foul play.

Their most likely suspect is a woman calling herself Navi Dalal, was untraceable. Investigators focus turn to the phone call Arjun received on the day he was on his way to Mumbai. They obtained the phone record of Arjun which identify phone calls from a residence in Vidica estate Mumbai, which was rented by a lady who was identify as Sahara Burman. She was not Arjun Khatri, but she was 5 feet one. Navi Dalal has described herself exactly that height. The call from Sahara Burman match the time when Navi Dalal allegedly phoned Arjun to set up a meeting in Mumbai. Navi was a fetishes figure, she never existed. She was supposed to set up the deal with Arjun Khatri. Navi Dalal was actually Sahara Burman. Investigators took Sahara Burman's pictures to the hotel where Arjun's credit cards has been used on January 28. The detectives asked to speak to the employee on duty in the morning in question. They checked the pay phone in the hotel that had been used with Arjun's credit card. Like the gas station, the phone required no signature from the customer, just the credit card. Heleena was working at the front desk on the morning in question. But she did not recognized the photo of Arjun Khatri. She did recall waiting for another customer that morning.

Around 2:00 am, a dark hair woman asked for a room. The hotel was fully booked so she used the pay phone several times to query other hotels. It was the same time Arjun Khatri credit card was used on the phone. Heleena described the woman living in her thirties with brown hair, and standing a little over 5 feet tall. The detectives showed her pictures of six women, and without hesitation Heleena quickly identify Sahara Burman being among the pictures. Sahara Burman is really the prime suspect. The detectives did have some evidence on her. They checked on the car rentals at the Mumbai airport, and found out that Sahara rented a car just shortly before Arjun arrived. Investigators found the car at the car rentals garage. The investigators for further investigation impounded the car. They found no trace of Arjun Khatri in the car. There was no physical evidence linking Sahara Burman to the missing businessman. The Imphal detectives began a 24/7 surveillance on Sahara. They followed the suspect for days to established a routine and determine her contacts. They learned that Sahara was dating a man name Samay Babu. Investigators began to tail Samay. Like Arjun, he also owned a bus company in Imphal, Manipur, but he is now living in Mumbai. The men have known each other rest of their lives.

Samay and Arjun are rivalry. The bus company are ten miles apart. Therefore, even though they both have their own contacts in their own businesses, they are always varying for the same contract and the same business. The phone record indicated recent calls to Arjun from Samay Babu's Mumbai's home. This seems strange for two men were fierce rivals. Detectives went to speak to the manager at Arjun's company. Meera Chadha said Arjun Khatri and Samay Babu used to be friends. But their business rivals made them enemies. She detailed the last time she had seen the men together. It was at an industry banquet on January 19, 1996. She and Arjun was talking when she saw Samay approaching. Angry at Arjun that he has stolen one of his bus contract. Samay threatened his rival. He said he is going to get him and put him under.

That could mean to put him out of business or he could kill him someday. Arjun took the threat seriously. Afterwards, Arjun would not go to any meeting Samay would attend, unless he has someone with him. Investigators contacted Samay and asked him if he had seen or spoken to Arjun recently. Samay denied ever calling Arjun on the day he embarked on his trip to Mumbai. Denying that phone calls has been made from his house to Arjun business, meaning something has been wrong. Investigators believe Samay and Sahara has probably killed Arjun Khatri. Nevertheless, they needed a stronger proof. They turned to an assistant state attorney. One of the first investigation tools that the investigators wants to use is wiretap. Therefore, you have to show a very compelling reason why you have to listen to someone's phone call.

Therefore, they drafted application to receive an order, allowing them to listen to Samay telephone conversation. Unfortunately, the investigators received very little phone conversation between Samay and Sahara. This is because Sahara was now living with Samay. If they were talking about Arjun's disappearance, it was not over the phone. In order to record any incriminating conversation, investigators will have to bug Samay's house. The investigators planted a listening device in Samay's house. They were outside the house watching and listening. They hope that the couple will discuss what happened to Arjun. Samay and Sahara were extremely courteous. Investigators noticed that if the couples want to talk, they would turn on the radio in the kitchen. By this, the investigators have several hours of tape with music and nothing on it. Once again, investigators came out empty handed.

With Arjun still missing, Samay and Sahara will elude authorities as long as they maintained their silence. In June of 1997, the Mumbai state agency believes that Samay and his girlfriend Sahara had murdered 57-year-old millionaire Arjun Khatri. However, investigators have little evidence against the couples, and Arjun's body was still missing. The police checked morgues in Mumbai where Arjun was believe missing and there were no identified body matching Arjun Khatri description. If Samay and Sahara has killed Arjun, they have covered their tracks well. In June of 1997, detective Rishi Bakshi of the Indian Special Task Force was assigned the case. The investigators believed Samay Babu killed Arjun over a disputed bus contract. Their best lead was Arjun's alleged meeting with Sahara. On June 13, 1997, Sahara Burman appeared before a Mumbai grand jury. When questioned by the state attorney, she was uncooperative and hostile. The judge cautioned her that if she did not answer she will be jailed for contempt, but Sahara ignored his warning.

The investigators believed that her refusal to cooperate means that she was involved in Arjun's disappearance. The gamble to Sahara backfired. Now that Samay closest ally was sitting behind bars, investigators have no potential witness to turn on the suspected murder. Lacking further leads a physical evidence. The case against the couple might never make it to trial. Detective Rishi and his team were determine to make this never to happen. The investigators from a reliable source heard that there is a witness who wanted to talk but was afraid of Samay's violence. Samay was a violent person and there could be a retaliation if this witness could talk. That witness was Ishan Chawla. A former pilot with the Indian air force and was one of Samay's best friend. The special task force interviewed him in his home in Mumbai just down the street from Samay's house. Ishan also owns a bus company in Panaji, Goa. He has been a commercial pilot after a decade of military service. Investigators believe that bond will help them develop Ishan as a witness.

Ishan told the special task force that his friendship with Samay has been strange recently. But he was reluctant in details between Samy relationship with Arjun. The task force believes Ishan knew something that will break the case wide open. They without no hesitation took it easy on Ishan. They gave him the freedom he needed and in their mind, they believe they have the man that has the answers and he is not telling them. They met with Ishan on many occasion and slowly won his confidence. They knew he was loyal to his friend Samay. But they felt his sense of honour and eventually they caused him to turn. Besides Ishan lingering doubts, the task force believes he was ready to talk. The investigators had to take the chance. Like Sahara, if Ishan had any part in the crime, his statement will not be used to prosecute him for murder. Five months after the disappearance of the multimillionaire Arjun Khatri, investigators have little evidence to support their allegation that Arjun was murdered by his business rival, Samay.

Chapter 3

Looking for a fresh lead, investigators decided to talk to Ishan, Samay best friend. Ishan has been reluctant to talk but after a month, the former Indian air force pilot sense of honour prevailed. He began by telling the investigators that Samay purchased a plane that year. Samay asked him to become his private pilot since he had experience flying fighter jets and commercial airlines. In exchange, he could use his plane as he wishes. In March of 1997, by staying in the hotel in Mumbai, providing repairs on the plane. Ishan was contacted by Samay. Samay said he needed Ishan to take the plane out on the ocean. Ishan explains that the aircraft will be grounded for several more days. He suggested they rented another plane. Samay insisted on using his own plane. He did not want anybody else to know about the flight.

Ishan asked why, and Samay told him that he had shot and killed Arjun Khatri, and that they had wrapped his body in plastic, and thrown him out on the ocean. And that the bag did not sink so he took a knife and stuck some holes on it, and the body did sink. Samay then told Ishan that he is worried because the body has surfaced. He wanted to fly over the area to make sure it have not surface. But Ishan refused. Ishan was shocked. He is also in the bus business with Samay and Arjun. But Ishan and Arjun were not friends. To Ishan, over a business rivalry, you do not kill somebody. According to Ishan, Samay murdered Arjun in his house. The former air force pilot confirmed what the investigators have been suspecting all along. It was the big break in the case. We were all waiting this moment for, without a body or murder weapon, they will need Ishan confession on tape. Ishan testimony was good, but in court, it will be his words against Samay. Ishan the prosecutor that he was reluctant to wear a wire. Ishan was afraid of Samay that he could kill him if he should wear a wire on him. The investigators promised him police protection.

He later agreed to wear the wire. The plan is to lure Samay to Ishan's house. The task force wired Ishan for sound and hid a video camera in the kitchen. When the equipment was in place, Ishan called Samay. He told him he has an idea regarding the issue of Arjun's death and he want to tell him what he should do. Samay said he would be right over. In case something went wrong, detective Rishi Bakshi will remain hidden in the house. When the investigation team saw Samay approaching, they quicly went into hiding. While waiting, they spotted some telephone repair people doing some repair work in the area. They quickly ordered them to leave to avoid blowing up the whole plan. They later made it up to their vehicle just before Samay showed up. The investigators tried to alert the men in the house, but they received no response. They have no way to know if the men in the house received their calls. Samay finally arrived and knocked at the door and Ishan opened it for him to come inside. Ishan led Samay into the kitchen and sat down on the table as planned. As the conversation begins, Samay was not speaking out. He would not talk loudly. He was pointing to the wall and saying, no, no, nobody knows. Whispering so that he could not be heard in Ishan's house.

Not that he suspected Ishan, but because he suspected that the police were everywhere. The detectives listen to Ishan and Samay from the car outside the house. They heard the discussion about what Ishan was to testify in court. Whether or not Ishan should lie for Samay. Ishan said to Samay if he refused to testify against him and be put in jail, whether he will come forward and tell the truth. Samay assured him that he would. Samay did not want to continue talking in Ishan's house. He led Ishan outside so that they can continue the conversation. This whole thing suppose to take place at Ishan's kitchen table, and no place else. So when you hear Samay saying, let's take a walk, the investigators were concern that he was walking Ishan out somewhere to eliminate him. Samay unknowingly walk Ishan into the surveillance team hideout. The team were inside their car parked about 80 feet from Samay and Ishan. They were wondering if the whole thing is going to be blown, should Samay saw the police vehicle. If the investigators are discovered, they might not be able to protect Ishan from Samay.

The investigators watches as both of them are trying to discuss the murder of Arjun outside of Ishan's house, close to their hideout. They feared what Samay might do if he should caught a glimpse of them. Before Samay could spot the surveillance team, Ishan stirred him away. The investigators now heard incriminating statements on tape but not a direct confession. They needed more. Samay accomplice, Sahara Burman remains in jail. She has been charged for contempt in court two months earlier for refusing to testify against Samay. The detectives interviewed Sahara's former roommate, and she said Sahara used to deal in cocaine, and the sedative Rohypnol. Rohypnol is odourless, and tasteless. Depending on the dose, it can relax a person or render them unconscious. The task force believes Sahara seduced Arjun with the drug. They suspected that Sahara and Arjun may have gone out for dinner and drinks, and then she was able to seduced him with the drug. Because Arjun will not knowingly and willingly go into Samay's house. Thinking all these information will pressure Sahara to talk as the task force met with her in jail. They told her that if she does not cooperate she would not have immunity. She could be charged with murder. Sahara remained silent despite the warning from the prosecutor. Sahara could have walked out of that jail cell any day simply by telling them what she knows about the case.

But she was tough enough and prefer to sit in jail on a civil contempt, believing she would soon be set free due to lack of enough concrete evidence against her. Despite Sahara's silence, the investigators press on. The assistant state attorney felt they are ready to arrest Samay. They have heard a witness to a confession who was very close to the defendant. They have a motive, a circumstantial evidence, being a very strong case. On August 30, the task force begins Arial surveillance on Samay. They ground surrounded around the perimeter of the suspects home. They made sure he was alone inside. That evening, the investigators positioned themselves by his door. They were waiting until he emerged to take him down the open. When he steps out with his dog, he was surrounded and arrested. The suspect offers no resistance. Seven months after Arjun's vanishes, Samay was arrested for kidnapping and murder of Arjun Khatri. With no physical evidence, prosecutor prepares for a difficult trial. When Samay's arrest hit the news, they receive a call from the man with information on the case. The man agreed to give a statement. Akhil Datta was Samay's son in-law. He said he received a call from Samay on January 28, the day

Arjun arrived in Mumbai. Samay asked him to come over to help him clean his house. He arrived on Tuesday 26. He said that Samay and Sahara has already began renovation of the house. The carpet has been ripped off and part of the wall has been removed. Akhil said Samay explained why. Samay told him that Arjun was at his house last Monday. Even Akhil knew the kind of relationship going on between Samay and Arjun that they were rivals and express some surprise why would Arjun be in his house. Samay said he does not want any trace of Arjun found in his house. Akhil swore that he never saw any blood. The task force asked Akhil if he questioned Samay of what happened. He said he could not want to ask or question his father in-law because he knew something bad had happened in his house. They used an industrial vacuum cleaner to clean the entire area. Akhil told the investigators that he and Samay disclosed the waste at a particular field. His statement collaborated Isham's story.

In the middle of August, investigators arrived at the field. They spent three days digging and searching until they found the carpets and other items buried in the field. They took all the items to the forensic department for analysis. Despite all these conclusions, the lab analyst were unable to match all these conclusive items linking to Samay's house. Investigators still have no physical evidence. The task force pressed on. They continue building a strong circumstantial case for the state prosecutor by further collaborating sanitation story about the cleanup. Just before time, investigators received disturbing news. Samay has hired someone to kill Isham. Samay knew that if he could prevent Isham from testifying against him, the prosecutor would have to drop the case. Eraly of 1997, kidnapping and muder suspect Samay Babu was held behind bar for the murder of Arjun Khatri. While he was behind bars, investigators learned that he has ordered the murder of the prime witness Isham Chawla.

As from that point the security for Isham was tremendously increased, and his family was taken to the federal protection program for security and protection. Samay trial began on January 20, 1999. Even without the victim's body, the Mumbai state attorney was confidence in the case. The prosecutor main witness Ishan Chawla recall all he knew about the murder of Arjun Khatri. The prosecutor filled in the gap, and detailed the events of January 28, 1997, the last day Arjun Khatri was seen alive. Samay's lover Sahara Burman picked up Arjun Khatri at the Mumbai airport that evening. She took him to Samay's house, on the pretense of meeting other business partners. Arjun was unaware that he has just step into the home of his biggest rival. While Sahara and Arjun discus the lucrative business deal, she dropped a capsule of Rohypnol into his drink. Arjun would not have noticed because the powerful sedative is tasteless, odourless, colourless and easily dissolvable. As the two talk, Sahara waited for the drug to take effect. As planned, Samay showed up and took over at that point. Arjun became unconscious as Sahara removed his wallet.

Later they used his credit cards to create a false trail for the police. Arjun was powerless due to the powerful sedative. Samay pull out a handgun, put it on Arjun's head and pulled the trigger. Arjun died on the spot. Samay had to get rid of the evidence. He wrapped the body and murder weapon in a plastic. He later dumped the body about 60 miles off shore. Ishan testified that Samay had to stabbed through the plastic several times to get it to sink. He then returned home to finish cleaning up. He tore out anything that is stained by blood. Using bleach, they scrubbed the entire area clean. Ishan testimony was boosted by powerful circumstantial evidence. Phone calls linking Samay and Arjun, Akhil sanitation story of the cleaning, and recordings from Ishan's house, was enough to convince the jury.

On February 10, 1999, the jury finds Samay Babu guilty of kidnapping and murder of Arjun Khatri. After Samay's trial, the prosecutor turns to Sahara Burman. Faced with murder charges, she formerly gave false testimony relating to Arjun's death. She was sentenced to 10 years in prison. Samay was sentenced to life in prison, for the kidnapping and murder of Arjun Khatri. Although Arjun Khatri's body was never recovered, but his killer and conspirator did not go free.

Killer In The Mist

Chapter 1

More than 30 years ago, on thanksgiving weekend, a teenager disappeared in Pasay, the Philippines. Pasay is a small community and everybody knows each other. They go to their local store diner for lunch or dinner, and they shop at the general store. They do not have to worry much about safety, as the town is very safe and most times they keep their doors unlock. Pasay, also called Rizal City, central Luzon, Philippines, situated on the eastern shore of Manila Bay. A major residential suburb of Manila (immediately north), it is well known for the nightclubs that line the waterfront along Roxas (formerly Dewey) Boulevard. Pasay is densely populated and highly commercialized. Araneta University (1946) is located in the city. Both the domestic and international airports are on its outskirts. Luzon, largest and most important island of the Philippines. It is the site of Manila, the nation's capital and major metropolis, and of Quezon City. Located on the northern part of the Philippine archipelago, it is bounded by the Philippine Sea east, Sibuyan Sea south, and the South China Sea west. To the north, the Luzon Strait separates Luzon from Taiwan.

Most of the island, a roughly rectangular area, lies north of Manila in a north-south orientation, while south of Manila are two peninsulas, Batangas and Bicol, which extend south and southeast, giving Luzon its irregular shape. Luzon's coastline, more than 3,000 miles (5,000 km) long, is indented by many fine bays and gulfs, including Lingayen Gulf and Manila Bay on the west and Lamon Bay and Lagonoy Gulf on the east. Luzon represents about one-third of the land area of the Philippines, and its greatest dimensions are 460 by 140 miles (740 by 225 km). There is a predominant north-south trend in its rivers and relief features. The important ranges are the Cordillera Central in the north; the Sierra Madre, following much of the east coast; and the Zambales Mountains on the central-western coast. Mount Pulog (9,612 feet [2,930 metres]) is the island's highest peak. Isolated volcanic cones such as the near-perfect and still-active Mayon Volcano (8,077 feet [2,462 metres]) are on Bicol Peninsula. Taal Lake is a crater lake, and Laguna de Bay is the largest (344 square miles [891 square km]) lake in the Philippines. The major rivers are Cagayan, Abra, Agno, Pampanga, and Bicol.

The City of Pasay is one of the cities and municipalities that make up Metro Manila in the Philippines. It is bordered on the north by the country's capital, Manila, to the northeast by Makati City, to the east by Taguig City, and Parañaque City to the south. In terms of area, Pasay City is the third smallest political subdivision in the National Capital Region. There are many conjectures as to the origin of the name "Pasay". In one version, the name of the municipality came from the wail of a brokenhearted swain. José and Paz were in love with each other and were intent on a life together, but José's father was a mere tenant of the hacienda of Paz's father. For this reason, their love was forbidden and José was ordered to stay away from Paz. Unable to bear her misfortune, Paz died.

At her funeral, the elite came to mourn and pray as José watched from a distance. As soon as everyone left, José dug a tunnel into the earth to be with Paz. Once joined, he let out a sharp and anguished cry "Paz-ay!" In sorrow and regret, the parents of Paz named their hacienda Paz-ay. In time, the town came to be known simply as Pasay. The version deemed to be most credible is that Pasay was named after a princess of the Namayan Kingdom, Dayang-dayang Pasay. The Namayan Kingdom was a confederation of barangays that began to peak in 1175 and extended from Manila Bay to Laguna de Bay. Dayang-dayang Pasay inherited the lands now comprising the territories of Culi-culi, Pasay and Baclaran. The royal capital of the kingdom was built in Sapa, known today as Santa Ana. The natives brought their products to the capital of Namayan. Trading flourished during the 12th to the 14th centuries. Merchants from Japan, China, Moluccas, Java, Borneo, Sumatra, India, Siam, and Cambodia came to trade with the natives.

Pasay's name may also have originated from the Spanish Paso hay meaning there is a pass. This referred to the paths cleared among the grass leading to the southern portions from Manila. In 1727, the name of the Pasay settlement was changed to Pineda in honor of Don Cornelio Pineda, a Spanish horticulturist who requested for guardias civiles for protection from bandits. The name Pineda, along with

Pasay, was used as the name of the place until the early 20th century. Most of the attractions in the city are on the CCP (Cultural Center of the Philippines) Complex, on which the massive main CCP building, Philippine International Convention Center (PICC), Tanghalang Francisco Balagtas (formerly Folk Arts Theater), Manila Film Center, Coconut Palace, Product Development and Design Center of the Philippines(PDDCP), Philippine Trade Training Center (PTTC), World Trade Center-Metro Manila(WTCMM), Cuneta Astrodome, and theme parks such as Star City, Nayong Pilipino, andBoom na Boom are all located. Terminal 2 and the recently opened Terminal 3 of the Ninoy Aquino International Airport, as well as the terminal of the Manila Domestic Airport is located in Pasay City. Villamor Airbase of the Philippine Air Force is also located here.

Other national government offices could be found in Pasay: Department of Foreign Affairs (DFA), Senate of the Philippines, the Philippine Department of Trade and Industry's export promotions agency – the Center for International Trade Expositions and Missions (CITEM) – located in the International Trade Complex's Golden Shell Pavilion, and the Overseas Workers Welfare Administration (OWWA). The main office of the Philippine National Bank, led by its president taipan Lucio Tan, is located in the City. Pasay City is home to the headquarters of the SM Group of Companies and the SM Mall of Asia, touted as the 2nd biggest mall in the Philippines which opened on May 21, 2006 and Mall of Asia Arena will be opened this 2012 which will be the biggest sports arena in the Philippines with the seat capacity of 20,000 and the new home of University Athletic Association of the Philippines and the National Collegiate Athletic Association. Also interesting is a budding strip of restaurants at the corner of EDSA Extension and Pres. Diosdado Macapagal Ave. It will also be the house of booming call center business industry in the Philippines due to vast land space available located in the reclamation area.

Living In Pasay City as a Foreigner: The honking of the jeepneys, the humid heat of the sun, and different types of people walking, chattering and noise may be the constant scenario of one of the busiest cities of the Philippines.

Looking at Pasay City through the eyes of a foreigner can be enticing to live. Living in Pasay City as a foreigner may be triggered by various reasons such as studies, for this is the city where you could find some of the oldest schools and universities in the country. Moving into one of the busiest cities of the Philippines, such as Pasay City, sounds exciting for it is just like having a capsulized city wherein everything you need is accessible such as the Ninoy international Airpot, Bus terminals, Supreme Court, the Philippines General Hospital, big universities, and one of the biggest mall which is the Mall of Asia. Before you start packing and readying your things, it may be wise if you take a few minutes to read and find out some details about what you will expect while living in Pasay City as a foreigner. You may be intrigued by the name of the city, Pasay. There are various versions of the story behind the name of the city, most of which are primarily based on local folklore.

Filipinos' way of transmitting their history, culture, and tradition is through telling stories or folklores. The name is part of the folklore of the place, which narrates that once the city was part of Namayan, it was the confederation of barangays. The Namayan ruler had given portions of territories to one of his sons named Pasay. Interestingly, in the other version, the daughter's name o the Rajah Sulayman of Manila was a recipient of the territories Culi-culi Pasay and Baclaran with a royal title Dayang-Dayang or the western title for a princess. So the princess's name was Pasay, and she was the princess of the Namayan Kingdom. Either version would attest that the city's name is from the name of a royal. The city may not be that big regarding the land area. It is considered the National Capital Region as the third smallest political subdivision.

The city can be seen as a capsulized city wherein it is just being divided into three districts which is the urban area. The second district is the Aeronautics Administration Complex. This is where the Ninoy Aquino International Airport and Villamor Airbase are included. The third district is the reclaimed area from Manila Bay. These are the places worth every minute of your time for living in Pasay City would entail fun, leisure, and education. It may not take to be an aviator to be delighted to visit this museum for this where the history of the Philippine Air Force (PAF) is enshrined where one can see on display are the different PAF aircraft models and types. Since you are already at the Villamor Airbase, you may want to take a stroll at the Villamor Golf Club, which is open for both the locals and foreigners. It is a 50-hectare golf course with the standard for championship tee for it has 18 hole par 72 courses.

It will be a walk through the mahogany and eucalyptus trees, and this golf club has superb facilities and amenities such as a café, swimming pool, and driving range. Though this may not be the biggest mall in the world compared to the mall in Dubai, the MOA is classified as the third largest mall globally. Moreover, with four hectares of floor area, one may be delighted with the mall's interconnected main buildings. Aside from the fact that it is located in Pasay City Bay, it also houses hundreds of restaurants, both local and foreign, and different retail outlets of clothes, bags, and shoes. If you miss the snow and want to have the feel of ice skating, you can enjoy that at SM MOA, for it has an Olympic-sized ice skating rink.

It also has a wide array of entertainment activities such as an IMAX theater, EXPLOREUM Science Center, SMX Convention Center, and an MOA Eye Ferris Wheel.

You can immediately jump off to a sun cruise when you are in the MOA complex, for this is the takeoff area for the sun cruise. The cruise that will take you back to the past of the Philippines as the boat ride will give you a tour of Corregidor Island. This historical Corregidor Island is strategically located at the entrance of Manila and is fortified to defend the city from any form of attack. As you tour, you will have a glimpse of how this island had played a crucial role during World War II that led the Japanese to be driven off the country. If the world underwater excites you as you want to feel the marine life, you may go to the Oceanarium. This is where you can closely look at the Philippine Marine Life as you can see the different types of fish underwater. The Oceanarium is considered the first theme park in the Philippines. The rates vary for it is entirely dependent on the type of packages and activities that you may want.

Chapter 2

Living in Pasay City as a foreigner will be fun, especially when you have kids to bring with you to Star City. There are various kiddie rides and an indoor playground, such as Dino Island and Winter Fun Land. Just for Php 70.00 entrance fee per head and Php 450.00, you and your family can enjoy the ride-all-you can. If you got the adrenalin rush for entertainment, you would love the Resorts World Manila, which is tagged as Pasay's one-stop for total entertainment. It is considered a friendly-tourist Newport Mall that caters to most high-end shops, and dining would be like choosing from about fifty dining outlets. In addition, it has a 24-hour movie theater and Newport Performing Arts Theater. When Saint John Paul, who was a Pope at that time, visited the Philippines in the year 1981, the Coconut Palace was being built which was made out of 100% Philippine indigenous materials such as coconut shells, Philippine hardwood, and banana fiber. The Coconut Palace, which is fondly called "Tahanang Pilipino," may be the epitome of Philippine architecture, and it is located at the Cultural Center of the Philippines (CPP) Complex.

Pasay City is in the top 31% of the least expensive cities, this is based on the ranking the 6340th from the 9294 global lists. In the Philippines, it ranked 8th among the 86 Cities. To summarise, to live comfortably as a foreigner in Pasay city you will need around $1300 – $1600 per month. Nonetheless, total costs can be much lower depending on your lifestyle and living arrangements. The city that caters to young professionals has affordable rates for eating out, such as $2.61 for a lunch menu. Although, a fast-food chain meal, it is around $2.74, dining out in a restaurant for two individuals will cost you $11.9. Cappuccino is priced at $1.86. Pasay City is one of the oldest cities in the Philippines and is dubbed a tourist-friendly city. Therefore, you can see a lot of foreigners enjoying life in Pasay City. Such friendliness of the locals would be an assurance that this place is safe for foreigners.

As one expat had exclaimed that "generally the Pasay area near MoA is safe. However, a few dark areas do exist – just avoid any dark, badly lit street". Same with other cities, you have to take precautions, for you may always expect some evildoers that have just been lurking around the corner. Pasay City crime is moderate to high in some areas in terms of statistics. However, petty crimes such as pickpocketing and scams are very common, so it's always best to be vigilant as a foreigner living in Pasay City. Dubbed as the city which is the "gateway to the world" for you to fly to different countries for it is where the Ninoy Aquino International Airport is located. It caters to international and domestic flights. It is one of the highly urbanized cities in south Manila.

The city is ideal for young or not-so-young professionals who are into the craze of professional growth. It is suited for a single individual and even for a family. There will be no dull moments when you live in the Pasay City premises, for you have many options ranging from historical travel to entertainment. It is also a starting point for your family's out-of-town adventure to the southern provinces like Cavite, Laguna, and Batangas. You can access the South Luzon Expressway and the Cavite Expressway in this city. The city is a fantastic place to live as it has a lot to offer foreigners; however, those who enjoy a peaceful, relaxed and quieter lifestyle may be more suited in other areas such as Davao or Iloilo City.

On November 24, 1989, Angela Ramos went out with her dog. The dog has returned but she has not. In addition, when she did not come back, her mother panicked. There was a massive hunt for her. It was three days later they found her. Her dead body was just floating lightly on a river. The police believes that there is a killer out there and the question is will this killer strikes again. For 25 years, there is no viable suspect in this case. However, the police did not give up. They kept on working, persisting and keep going. Angela is dead but the case is not going to die. In June 2013, there was an unexpected break. Amazingly enough there were two women talking in the water park. They gave the police a break in the case. Back then, detective Joshua Santos led the search for Angela Ramos, moving up the river in a zodiac boat. He later found Angela floating on the river and wearing only her running shoes.

Joshua and the small community in Pasay are still emotional even 30 years later. Jacob Cruz was Angela's high school basketball coach. He gave a memorial service attended by nearly a thousand people. He has been her mentor after her parents divorced. She was a basketball player, cheerleader, top student and an aspiring airline pilot, Angela Ramos truly stood out. She wanted to be very good to the best at everything she does. All that promise ended in 1989. When the college freshman came from central Pasay University for thanksgiving, the day after the big holiday meal in the house, Angela set out on the last job of her life. With her German shepherd, dog Max. Detective Daniel Lopez, who was a deputy back then, has put the pieces together from the few people who saw her that day. The last person to see Angela alive was a man on a pickup truck who pulled up by the road and Angela ran right in front of him. Heading in the direction to her home about a 8 of a mile from where the truck was.

Investigators believed that the attacker had kicked the dog into a ditch before adopting Angela. He then sexually assaulted her about three and half miles away from where she was jogging. Afterward she tried to flee. A scenario suggested by the scratches on her arms. She managed to escape from the kidnapper and was running away. Nevertheless, the attacker chased and caught her. He knocked her on the head, killed her and dumped her into the river, so she drowned and died. When the police did the autopsy, they were able to discover a male DNA from Angela. The male DNA discovered was a semen, suggesting a sexual attack. John Flores was a local technician seen in the area that day. The police got a warrant to obtain his DNA and he was ruled out as it did not match. The police interviews every person of interest including Angela's boyfriend Mark Valdez. In all, some 30 local men gave DNA samples and non-matched. The case went cold and the murderer turned like a dark cloud in the community for the next two decades.

Then almost 25 years later, a new suspect emerged. He had lived right in Angela's neighbourhood. His name was not even on the radar. Alexa

Ramos, Angela's mother have spent years hunting for the murderer of her teenage daughter. Though the case is lacking some progress but detective Daniel Lopez had never given up. By 2009, he was the lead investigators on this unsolved case. He began going through the case file. Going over all leads and old suspects. He started going through who was interviewed and who was talked to. Daniel noticed that a local drug dealer name Angelo Santos has been questioned because he told people that he might know who murdered Angela Ramos. Although his DNA did not match the crime scene, detective Daniel still want to talk to him again. In 2010, he travelled all the way to Cambodia where Angelo Santos now lived to question him. But a feeling was not evidence. Angelo felt he knew who murdered Angela but the police needed a concrete evidence and not assumption. Three years later the police got a tip that send them into a new direction.

Chapter 3

Coming from all places, a pair of mum chatting in a water park. It was June 2013, Julia Delos and Lea Diaz was being interviewed in the water park about what they know about Angela Ramos murder case. They had kept it secret for years because of the weight of the matter and they do not want to get involved. But after many years later, they decided to get involved. They gave the suspect name as Franco Torres. The two women gave a disturbing testimony of their experiences with Franco Torres before the murder of Angela. How he tried to rape them but did not succeed. Franco lives in a home less than 2 miles from Angela's house. Franco along with his father and brother had never been asked to give DNA sample. The police overlooked them. And for the past 20 years, Franco has been living a quiet life in the nearby community.

Franco is married with three children, and driving a delivery truck for a bakery. The police decided to pay Franco a visit. When asked about Angela, Franco pretended that he did not even remembered her. At least not at first. Later he just looked up and said, Angela, Angela, Angela, oh yes, that was the girl they found dead in the river. The police asked Franco for a saliva samples to get his DNA. But Franco thought to himself that if he should give out his DNA he could be caught and go to jail. Therefore, he refused. The police began trailing Franco anywhere he goes. They hope that Franco will throw away an item with DNA on it, but no luck. The investigation stalled yet again. Until the police received an unexpected helping hand. 24 long years have passed without an arrest. The police finally have a prime suspect. Back in 1989, Franco Torres lived down the road from Angela's house, and she often jugged passed his house on her regular running route, which is how he fixated on her.

Investigators knew Angela did not jugged by the Torres house the day she disappeared. However, Franco was not at home then. The police wanted to know more about it. They got some background from his younger brother Carlos Torres. As kids, they play around together like most brothers. Franco has always been a loner. However, as a teenager, he began to recall deeper issues. Social interaction has never been natural to him. In his high school days, when his girlfriend broke up with him, he almost kill himself with a handgun. He fired some shots into the air several times. From that, time people close to Franco noticed a change in him. Franco got married young at 22, just six weeks after Angela's murder. He got married to Liza Torres. According to Liza, Franco was a controlled and abusive husband. He had often times abused Liza. Nevertheless, Liza stuck with him. She almost divorced him but was afraid of losing custody of her kids and decided to stay in the marriage despite Franc's domestic violence.

However, the detectives believes that they have had their killer but have to prove it. The wanted to cast a wider net to the potential suspect to be sure they are on the right part. Investigators got DNA from three dozens more men from the area but Franco Torres would not cooperate. So the police called the bakery where he works and spoke with his boss Marian Ramirez. Marian said that Franco is very provocative and have low regard for women, so they usually stay away from him. As Marian chatted with the investigators she realized they were looking at Angela's murder and figured out what they were really after. Marian asked the police if they wanted DNA, and the police said yes. She promised to get it for them. She kept an eye on Franco day after day watching if he will discard anything that might have a saliva on it. It took three long months and finally he saw him throw away a plastic cup, and later a coke can. She picked them up and gave them to the police. After the DNA examination in the forensic lab, they finally got a match. Franco DNA matches the DNA of the person's semen that assaulted and killed Angela Ramos. The police was so excited that it was like crying with tears coming out from their eyes. After so many years, they finally got Angela's killer. After the DNA match, the police paid another visit to Franco at work.

The police asked him if he have had any relationship with Angela, he said no. The police asked him again if he ever kissed or have an affair with Angela, he said never. Then the police said then why will his DNA be inside her. Franco went from denial to challenge the police on how they got his DNA. Right after that conversation, on December 12, 2017, 28 years after Angela has been found dead, the police arrested

50-year-old Franco Torres in the bakery-parking lodge. He was charged with kidnapping, rape and murder. Later that day the police came knocking at Alexa Roams door the mother of late Angela Ramos. That happens to be her birthday. They told her that they have gotten the murder of Angela. She was so happy to hear that. It was like to her a dream. Angela's older sister too was overwhelm. Detective Daniel called Marian with the news. Marian first thought was about Angela. It was a big lead thinking they had their man and convicting him in the law court.

Franco was asking the police if they are trying to get him to admit to something he did not do. He said that he was innocent and that he has a secret that explain everything. He said he just want to let them know that he slept with Angela. For prosecutor Jose Domingo It is a long road to justice. He said Angela was a good kid and this would not have happen to her. Jose was 44 when Angela was murdered. Now at 73, he has come out of retirement and insisted he should not be paid as he leads the prosecution team in this deeply personal case. After 30 years of headache, fear and frustration, the trial of Angela accused killer finally begins. The state case is simple. According to the defense attorney, Dennis Sanchez said that Franco Torres is not guilty. Dennis said Franco did not kidnapped anyone and did not raped anyone and certainly did not killed anyone. He further said that Franco and Angela were both having sex willingly and that cannot be term as rape. Franco also said that it was more a friendship thing. Him and Angela just talked and grew up. Dennis also said that DNA could only tell you that there was a contact. As the trial goes on in the court, Nora Castro the forensic analyst was called upon.

She said the semen could have been deposited two days before Angela's death. Franco ex-wife Liza was also in court to testify. Liza had divorced Franco after his arrest ad claims to having an affair with Angela. Liza also said she witnessed Franco asking his mother to lie for him. To point the finger at his own dad. Franco's father had died more than a decade earlier. But his mother refused and said no. Franco's brother Carlos Torres was also called to testify in court. Carlos told the court that Franco told him that he slept with Angela a decade ago and that he Carlos should lie to the police that he also slept with Angela. Franco also said to his mother that the police are lying and everybody is after him. He needs a strong alibi or he is going to prison. Also that Franco told her mother to lie that they were at Christmas shopping and Carlos should do what he can to defend him. But the defense attorney said that the investigation is based on false assumption. The reason being that Franco and Angela are not being seen together does not mean that there was no relationship going on between both of them. He was on the side of the defendant and prime suspect Franco Torres.

He also stated that the investigators called it a sexual assault. After 26 years and six months on Angela's murder, the jury finally gave its verdict. Franco Torres was found guilty of kidnapping, rape and murder. Six weeks later, it was time for sentencing. Before the sentencing, Franco mother was allowed to speak in the court. She said that her son Franco never blamed his father for the death of Angela. She also said that her son was innocent and not guilty of his crime. The convicted murderer Franco Torres who's DNA has sealed his faith spoke in court for the first time. Franco said that he is 100 percent innocent of the crime and that he has not received a fair trial. He was sentenced to 27 years in prison. He could not get life sentence because the prosecutors did not charged him premeditated murder. They could not get concrete evidence to do that. Franco's wife was asked by the prosecutor how she felt about the judgement.

She said she believed Franco was guilty and that she had lived in prison for 28 years with him and now is his turn. For Alexa, she once thought she will never see justice but Franco's sentenced gave her some relief and great joy. Julia and Lea were happy for the role they played in putting Franco away.

About the Author

Bright Mills

Best selling author Bright Mills is a writer, an engineer and a historian from Nigeria. He has a degree in Information Technology. He is a creative writer and have written so many books in Fiction and non fiction. His books have received starred reviews weekly, library journal, and Book list. He promises to pull heart strings, offer a few laughs, and share tidbits of tantalizing history. His work has been praised by many.

www.ingramcontent.com/pod-product-compliance
Lightning Source LLC
LaVergne TN
LVHW041556070526
838199LV00046B/2002